W9-CJS-211

BATMAN™ BATTLES THE JOKER

Adapted by Laurie S. Sutton
Based on the screenplay *Monster Mayhem*
written by Heath Corson
Batman created by Bob Kane with Bill Finger

Simon Spotlight
New York London Toronto Sydney New Delhi

Based on the screenplay by Heath Corson

Copyright © 2016 DC Comics.
BATMAN and all related characters and elements © & ™ DC Comics
and Warner Bros. Entertainment Inc. (s16) SISC37472

This book is a work of fiction. Any references to historical events, real people, or real
places are used fictitiously. Other names, characters, places, and events are products of
the author's imagination, and any resemblance to actual events or places or persons, living or
dead, is entirely coincidental.

SIMON SPOTLIGHT
An imprint of Simon & Schuster Children's Publishing Division
1230 Avenue of the Americas, New York, New York 10020
This Simon Spotlight edition December 2016. All rights reserved, including the right of
reproduction in whole or in part in any form. SIMON SPOTLIGHT and colophon are
registered trademarks of Simon & Schuster, Inc. For information about special
discounts for bulk purchases, please contact Simon & Schuster Special
Sales at 1-866-506-1949 or business@simonandschuster.com.
Manufactured in the United States of America 1116 LAK
10 9 8 7 6 5 4 3 2 1
ISBN 978-1-4814-8014-7 (hc)
ISBN 978-1-4814-8013-0 (pbk)
ISBN 978-1-4814-8015-4 (eBook)

CHAPTER 1

In the dark of night, two evil inmates escaped from the Arkham Asylum and ran to freedom . . . to the streets of Gotham City. Usually, people would take one look at Solomon Grundy and Silver Banshee and run the other way, but tonight was different. It was Halloween. People thought they were wearing costumes, just like everyone else.

A man dressed as a rock star bumped into

the massive Grundy, took one look at him, and said, "Zombie wrestler! Nice one!" before walking away.

"Grundy love Halloween!" Grundy told Banshee. They were standing in the middle of the street when a red convertible drove up, full of

people dressed like super heroes. "Get out of the street!" said the driver.

"Heroes. Figures!" Banshee said to Grundy. Then she shouted at the super heroes, "Well, I *hate* your costumes, and so does my friend!"

Grundy lifted the car and dumped its passengers onto the street. Then he and Banshee jumped into the convertible and drove off.

Soon police vehicles chased them with sirens screaming. Silver Banshee screamed back. Her sonic blast hit the police cars like a sledgehammer and made them crash.

Nightwing and Green Arrow noticed the chase from a rooftop and took action! Green Arrow shot an arrow at the stolen car, which made Grundy, who was driving, lose control. Banshee launched a sonic blast back at Green Arrow.

"Jump!" Nightwing yelled to Green Arrow. They escaped the blast just in time!

That's when the Batmobile joined the chase. Red Robin used the car's computer to find out who was driving the convertible.

"Positive ID. It's Solomon Grundy and Silver Banshee," he said.

"Let's see if they want a trick or a treat," the Dark Knight said as he drove in front of the villains' car.

Grundy made the convertible take a sharp turn to escape. That's when Nightwing dropped down from a rooftop into the backseat. He fought Silver Banshee as Green Arrow drove up on his motorcycle!

They all sped toward a tunnel, with Batman and Red Robin close behind. Once Grundy, Banshee, Nightwing, and Green Arrow had made it inside, Banshee used a sonic scream to collapse the entrance so the Batmobile couldn't enter.

"Now what?" asked Red Robin.

The Dark Knight pushed a button on the

dashboard of the Batmobile. The front of the car opened up, and a huge drill began to cut through the rubble.

Inside the tunnel, Nightwing and Green Arrow were hit by sticky green globs of goo.

"No!" Green Arrow shouted as the goo erupted into Scarecrow's fear gas, knocking the heroes unconscious.

Scarecrow came out from the shadows. He was furious with Grundy and Banshee.

"I told you to head directly to the meeting place. No antics. No shenanigans," Scarecrow said. He hit the convertible with his fists. "This is the definition of shenanigans."

Grundy and Banshee looked glum as Scarecrow took the driver's seat. They sped out of the tunnel, leaving the heroes behind.

Soon after, Batman and Red Robin made it into the tunnel. Nightwing and Green Arrow were just beginning to wake up from what felt like a nightmare.

"There's residue from Scarecrow's fear gas," the Dark Knight said.

Red Robin's eyes widened. "Scarecrow, Silver Banshee, and Solomon Grundy are all working together?"

It sounded like the nightmare was just beginning.

While the real-life Batman battled super-villains on the streets of Gotham City, video game designer Gogo Shoto was using a virtual-reality game he invented to pretend to be Batman.

He was fighting virtual villains when his secretary interrupted him. Well, he *thought* it was his secretary, but then she tried to punch him, and her fist went through the wall. *WHAAAAM!*

Shoto fled to the computer core in his office and sent out a digital distress call. Batman saw a giant Bat-Signal on an electronic billboard and arrived just in time to see the secretary turn into a giant blob of clay: Clayface! Before Batman could stop him, Clayface stuffed Shoto into his gooey body, sprouted pterodactyl-like wings, and flew out the window. Batman deployed his glider cape and followed close behind, but Clayface escaped down a manhole with Shoto.

CHAPTER 2

At S.T.A.R. Labs, Police Commissioner Gordon had learned there was a break-in at an experimental artificial intelligence lab, but the security footage was too scrambled to see who did it. He asked Cyborg for high-tech help to clear the footage, and the culprits were revealed: Scarecrow and Banshee!

"Why would a couple of fright freaks spend

Halloween stealing an AI? Identity theft? Digital robbery?" Cyborg wondered. He decided to call Batman for help.

The Dark Knight had another idea. "It must be for someone else," he concluded. "Keep your eyes peeled, Cyborg."

Nightwing was nearby, and he called Batman on his comm as he watched Grundy break into a power plant. Inside, Grundy knocked out all the security guards and stole an atomic battery the size of a barrel. He lifted it onto his shoulder, walked out of the building, and put it into the back of an ice cream truck that was waiting outside. Nightwing was waiting too and hit Grundy with electrified batons.

"Pretty re*volt*ing, eh, Grundy?" Nightwing quipped.

"Hey! I'll do the jokes around here," a voice inside the truck declared.

Nightwing knew that voice! "The Joker? Uh-oh."

Grundy battled Nightwing as the Joker drove away . . . with the atomic battery.

Batman used his glider wings to sneak up

on the Joker's ice cream truck from the air, but the Joker saw him coming. He steered the ice cream truck off the side of an overpass, landed on the road below, and zoomed off in another direction.

Batman switched from glider to Batcycle to continue the chase. Batman launched Batarangs, but the Joker swerved the truck out of the way.

"You can't outrun me, Joker," Batman declared.

"Outrun you? Where's the sport in that? I'm waiting for *him*," the Joker laughed.

Solomon Grundy appeared on a motor-cycle and knocked Batman off the highway. By the time the Dark Knight climbed back up, the two villains were gone.

Later, in an abandoned carnival ware-house, the Joker and his crew welcomed their "guest."

"Wakey, wakey, Gogo Shoto," the Joker said.

The game designer woke up to see Clayface, Scarecrow, Banshee, Grundy, and the Joker standing in front of him.

"Please don't hurt me." Gogo gulped.

"Hurt you? Don't talk twaddle, genius," the Joker replied. "I need you. I'm going to play an amazing practical joke on Gotham City, and I need your help to do it!"

CHAPTER 3

In the Batcave beneath Wayne Manor, the Dark Knight studied files on Scarecrow, Grundy, Clayface, and Banshee.

"That's a frightful four if I've ever seen one," said Red Robin.

"Why join forces?" Batman wondered. "And why kidnap the head of a video game company?"

It was a puzzle, and Batman didn't have all the pieces yet.

"I heard a rumor that in his next game you'll be able to be . . . Batman," Red Robin said.

"Multiple Batmans?" asked Alfred, who had just walked in. "Terrifying." Then he reminded Batman about the museum gala happening that night.

As Bruce Wayne, Batman was expected to attend, but he had a bad feeling about the party and thought he might need help. "Tell Dick and Oliver I want them there too," Batman told Alfred, referring to his friends Nightwing and Green Arrow by their real names.

At the museum gala, Cyborg was the guest of honor. He had used his radar to discover a rare gem, which was on display. The Inca Rose Stone, as it was called, was also an excellent energy conductor.

As Bruce Wayne spoke with a guest, he spotted other super heroes and went over to talk strategy.

"You expecting Mr. Funny Business tonight?" Oliver Queen asked Bruce and Dick Grayson.

"After stealing a hacker, an AI, and a battery, an energy conductor fits the pattern,"

Bruce replied. "Stay alert. The Clown is up to something."

Moments later the Joker made a grand entrance.

"I don't want any trouble," he said. Then he pointed to the life-size model of a dinosaur behind him. "Now, my friend—he loves trouble!"

The giant dinosaur roared and came to life, chasing the guests of the gala! Cyborg fired his sonic cannon at the dinosaur, but the pulse passed through it. Then the dinosaur was hit by an explosive arrow. It stumbled backward and, in the confusion, turned back into Clayface.

In the chaos, the Joker grabbed the Incan gem and ran.

Outside, the Joker escaped on his purple motorcycle, and Clayface crammed into the stolen convertible with Grundy, Scarecrow, and Banshee.

Soon Batman was chasing them on the Batcycle. Nightwing and Green Arrow followed in the Batmobile, Red Robin rode a Cyberbat like an airborne skateboard, and Cyborg rocketed overhead.

Then the Joker pulled out a handheld comm and spoke a simple command: "Do it."

He had activated a computer virus! All the lights in Gotham City stopped working,

and so did the Batcycle and Batmobile. Red Robin's Cyberbat failed in midair. Cyborg fell to the ground, and Clayface captured him. The creepiest thing of all was that as the Joker's virus infected Cyborg, he could not stop laughing.

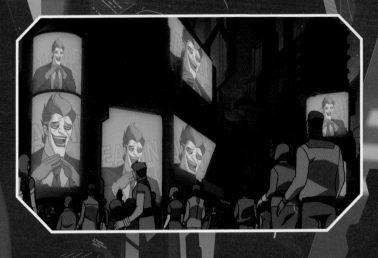

CHAPTER 4

Suddenly all the screens and TV monitors in Gotham City turned on and showed the Joker.

"Citizens of Gotham City," he announced. "As you can see, my digital laughing virus has infected every piece of technology in the entire city. Power plants. Traffic lights. Everything on the digital grid now belongs to me. Nothing around here works unless I say it

works, which makes me king of Gotham City!"
he said, putting on a crown. As he announced
the new rules of Gotham City, the citizens
watched in fear.

Back in the Batcave, Batman, Green Arrow, Nightwing, and Red Robin worked to figure out where the Joker was hiding. Wherever he was, they guessed he was using energy from the Incan gem to boost the signal for his TV broadcasts.

Samples of clay from Clayface contained debris that pointed to beach sand. An audio recording of the Joker's TV broadcast revealed a bell ringing on a navigational buoy.

Then Batman realized that the Joker's motorcycle was part of an old carnival ride, and all the clues fit together. The Joker's lair was in the abandoned fairgrounds on the Old Gotham Pier!

At the pier, Green Arrow stood on top of the Ferris wheel and fired a gas arrow into the Joker's lair. The villains ran outside, gasping for air, but Banshee spotted Green Arrow and sent a sonic shriek toward him. He leaped aside, and Banshee went after him as the rest of the villains ran off to look for the other super heroes.

That's when Red Robin sneaked inside the lair. He found Cyborg unconscious and hooked up to the stolen atomic battery and a bunch of computers. Red Robin couldn't disconnect him.

Then he heard a muffled call for help. It was Gogo Shoto! Red Robin freed the game designer just as Clayface stomped in.

"I'll pound you into mush!" Clayface shouted.

Red Robin tossed a couple of small spheres into the villain's open mouth, where they released gas. Clayface belched and then fell over, defeated.

Meanwhile, Green Arrow was in trouble.

Silver Banshee used her screams to smash the Ferris wheel out from under him! He landed on the boardwalk to face her with an arrow drawn. She broke his bow, but he knocked her to the ground and escaped.

Batman stood in a boat on the Tunnel of Love ride and waited as Solomon Grundy jumped down the line of boats to reach him!

Batman leaped onto a ledge to escape, and Grundy fell into the water.

Grundy growled, "This won't stop me."

Batman used a Batarang to cut an electrical cable and then used it to knock out Grundy with a powerful shock.

Since his bow was broken, Green Arrow grabbed a baseball from a carnival game and used it to knock Silver Banshee out. Then he assembled an extra bow he had for emergencies.

The super heroes brought the defeated villains to the Joker's lair and tied them up, but the most evil villain of all was still on the loose.

CHAPTER 5

The Joker rode up on his motorcycle with an insane grin and faced the Dark Knight.

"We've taken down your team. You can't beat us all by yourself," Batman said.

"See, with my computer virus, I control the computers in your vehicles," the Joker replied. "So this showdown isn't with me. It's with *them*. . . ."

The Batwing, the Batmobile, Ace the

Bat-Hound, and Cyborg appeared, and the Batwing fired rockets at the super heroes. They jumped aside and split up to take on the rogue tech.

Nightwing leaped onto the Batwing as it flew past him. He tried to get to the control box on the back of the aircraft to pull out its control chip, but the Batwing was trying to buck him off. Then Nightwing punched the control box with his fist, and the Batwing fell out of the sky and landed in the Gotham River. So did Nightwing!

Batman hung on to the Batmobile as it zoomed through the streets. The vehicle finally threw him off and launched small rockets at him. Batman jumped down a manhole in the street and, from underneath, ripped a leak in the car's fuel line. He ignited the trail of fuel with a Batarang, and the rogue Batmobile exploded.

Green Arrow led Ace, the cyber wolf, on a chase up the side of a roller coaster, and Ace used his metal claws to climb up. Green Arrow slid down the roller coaster tracks and jumped to the ground, but Ace chased him into a dead end. Then Green Arrow spotted the car of a carnival ride hanging above Ace and used his

new bow to shoot arrows at the wires until they snapped. The car fell on Ace, and Green Arrow escaped!

Meanwhile, Cyborg was being controlled by the Joker's computer virus, and he shot laser blasts at Red Robin.

"You can beat this. I know you can," Red Robin told his friend.

"Get out of here. I'm not responsible for my actions," Cyborg moaned.

"Maybe we can help," Batman said from a nearby rooftop. He and the rest of the team worked together to flood the street Cyborg was standing in and then send an electric shock through the water. Cyborg fell down, alive but unconscious.

Batman returned to the Batcave, where Gogo Shoto had valuable information for him.

"Joker's got an AI to deliver the digital virus he had me build," Gogo said. "I can build an interface to physically hack the AI if you can find the hard drive containing it."

Suddenly a Joker TV broadcast appeared on the Batcave monitors. As the trickster rambled about a parade to be held in his honor, Batman noticed the computers in the background of the news station's set.

"The AI is in the control room mainframe," Batman realized. "Joker's going to try to send this virus worldwide."

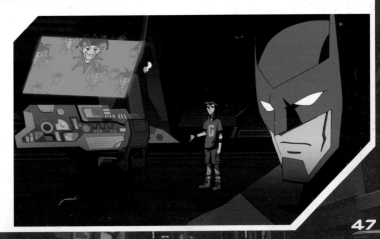

CHAPTER 6

Batman entered the news station as silent as a shadow. The Joker didn't notice him as he used Gogo's device to hack into the AI and . . . enter a virtual-reality world imagined by the Joker, who appeared as a digital avatar.

"You're in my world now," the Joker's avatar said as he made Batman morph into "Fatman"! Then the Joker's avatar split into multiple Jokers, all chasing Batman.

Batman willed himself back into his normal form and then created a mechanical T. Rex, setting it loose on the multiple Jokers. He was just stalling for time until he could hack the Joker's virus and infect it with a virus of his own.

"Upload complete," the AI announced overhead.

After that, it didn't take long for Batman to turn all but one of the Joker avatars into Batman avatars.

"Looks like your virus caught a virus," Batman said to the main Joker avatar. Then he escaped the virtual world and came back to reality.

Meanwhile, at the TV station, the real Joker was counting down the seconds until his computer virus would infect the whole world.

The clock hit zero, but nothing happened! Then a malfunction alert flashed across the Joker's computer, and all the computer systems in Gotham City rebooted.

Cyborg returned to normal and was shocked to find out that he had tried to fight his super hero friends.

Everyone was hopeful until the Joker appeared on a TV billboard to gloat. "You didn't really think I'd transmit my digital virus from only one location, did you?"

A new countdown flashed on every TV screen. Batman and his team had ten minutes to find the second transmitter.

That's when the Joker, in his mech suit, stomped through a parade of people wearing Joker masks. Cyborg attacked the Joker, but he got slammed into a building.

Then Batman, who had left the news station, flew a World War II fighter plane toward the Joker, using the low-tech machine guns to fire at him. Nightwing and Red Robin rode vintage motorcycles and threw explosives at the mech suit's metal head until it cracked. Finally, Green Arrow rumbled around the corner in a tank to finish the job.

The mech suit was destroyed, but the real Joker wasn't finished. He rocketed into the sky in his jet-powered stealth suit.

Cyborg and Batman chased the Joker above Gotham City.

Suddenly, Batman realized that Cyborg was the second transmitter! He told Cyborg, "Joker must have the gem attached to you somehow!"

Cyborg scanned his systems and saw the gem imbedded in his arm circuits. The only way to keep the gem from transmitting the digital virus was to attach it to the central core of the Joker's battle suit.

FOREIGN OBJECT IDENTIFIED

00:30

Cyborg punched through the Joker's battle suit, linking the gem to the suit's circuitry. The Joker's battle suit exploded, and he fell into the Gotham River.

The people of Gotham City were safe from the Joker's computer virus and his cronies. Those villains were all in police custody, but the Joker was still missing.

"We combed the river. No sign of the Joker," Nightwing reported.

"He'll be back," Batman replied.

On the other side of the river, the Joker walked out of the water and down a country road, already planning his next evil scheme!

GREAT RIVER REGIONAL LIBRARY
ST. CLOUD www.griver.org

3 2020 0446 5304

Adapted by
**LAURIE S.
SUTTON**

IT'S HALLOWEEN IN GOTHAM CITY,

but Batman™ isn't getting any treats. The Joker™ is unleashing a computer virus that could take control of all technology in the city, making it cackle and obey his every command! And he isn't working alone: The city's spookiest villains are working for the Joker and keeping Batman busy by going on a crime spree. Can Batman—and his pals Green Arrow™, Cyborg, Nightwing™, and Red Robin™—keep Gotham City from being tricked into becoming Jokertown?

Look for more books about
BATMAN™
at your favorite store!

010-241915

WATCH
WEBISODES ON
BATMANUNLIMITED.COM

Simon Spotlight
Simon & Schuster, New York

Visit us at SIMONANDSCHUSTER.COM/KID

ISBN 978-1-4814-8013-0   **$5.99 U.S./$7.99 Can.**

50599

9 781481 480130

Copyright © 2016 DC Comics.
BATMAN and all related characters and elements
© & ™ DC Comics and Warner Bros. Entertainment Inc.
DC LOGO: ™ & © DC Comics. WB SHIELD: ™ & © WBEI.
(s16)
SISC37472

1216

EBOOK EDITION ALSO AVAILAB